Dear Parent:
Your child's love of reading starts here!

Every child learns to read in a different way and at his or her own speed. Some go back and forth between reading levels and read favorite books again and again. Others read through each level in order. You can help your young reader improve and become more confident by encouraging his or her own interests and abilities. From books your child reads with you to the first books he or she reads alone, there are I Can Read Books for every stage of reading:

SHARED READING
Basic language, word repetition, and whimsical illustrations, ideal for sharing with your emergent reader

BEGINNING READING
Short sentences, familiar words, and simple concepts for children eager to read on their own

READING WITH HELP
Engaging stories, longer sentences, and language play for developing readers

READING ALONE
Complex plots, challenging vocabulary, and high-interest topics for the independent reader

ADVANCED READING
Short paragraphs, chapters, and exciting themes for the perfect bridge to chapter books

I Can Read Books have introduced children to the joy of reading since 1957. Featuring award-winning authors and illustrators and a fabulous cast of beloved characters, I Can Read Books set the standard for beginning readers.

A lifetime of discovery begins with the magical words "I Can Read!"

Visit www.icanread.com for information
on enriching your child's reading experience.

I Can Read Book® is a trademark of HarperCollins Publishers.

Superman: Superman Versus Mongul
SUPERMAN and all related characters and elements are trademarks of DC Comics © 2011. All rights reserved.
Manufactured in the U.S.A. No part of this book may be used or reproduced in any manner whatsoever without written permission except
in the case of brief quotations embodied in critical articles and reviews. For information address HarperCollins Children's Books, a
division of HarperCollins Publishers, 10 East 53rd Street, New York, NY 10022.
www.icanread.com

Library of Congress catalog card number: 2010926431
ISBN 978-0-06-188518-1
Typography by John Sazaklis

14 15 16 17 18   LP/WOR   10 9 8 7 6 5 4   ❖   First Edition

I Can Read!™

READING WITH HELP 2

SUPERMAN™

Superman
versus Mongul

by Michael Teitelbaum
pictures by MADA Design, Inc.

SUPERMAN created by Jerry Siegel and Joe Shuster

HARPER
An Imprint of HarperCollinsPublishers

CLARK KENT

Clark Kent is a
newspaper reporter.
He is secretly Superman.

LOIS LANE

Lois Lane is a
reporter. She works
for the *Daily Planet*
newspaper.

JIMMY OLSEN

Jimmy Olsen is a
photographer. He works
with Clark and Lois at the
Daily Planet.

SUPERMAN

Superman has
many amazing powers.
He was born on the
planet Krypton.

MONGUL

Mongul is a powerful
alien. He wants
to take over Earth.

WARWORLD

Warworld is Mongul's
giant spaceship.
It is the size of a planet.

A giant spaceship moved quickly

toward Earth.

The spaceship was called Warworld.

An alien named Mongul

was in charge of Warworld.

Mongul was very powerful.

He planned to take over Earth.

Inside Warworld,
Mongul sat in his control chair.
"Soon this planet will be mine!"
he said.

At US Army headquarters,

Warworld appeared on the screen.

"What is that?" one general asked.

"An alien spaceship," said another.

"Prepare for an attack!"

At the *Daily Planet* newspaper,
Lois Lane stepped into
Clark Kent's office.

Clark was looking out the window.

"Stop staring into space,"

Lois joked,

"and do some work."

But Clark wasn't listening to Lois.

His super-hearing had picked up

the sound of explosions.

"What's wrong?" Lois asked.

But Jimmy Olsen rushed in
before Clark could answer.
"An alien is attacking the city!"
Jimmy cried.

Clark changed in a flash.

"This looks like a job for Superman!"
he said.

Superman flew over Metropolis.

Below, he spotted Mongul.

The army was battling the alien.

But Mongul was so strong,

nothing hurt him.

A crowd of people ran in panic.

Superman spotted his friends.

"It's Jimmy and Lois!" he cried.

"They must be here to cover the story!"

Jimmy and Lois were standing
right in the alien's path.
"I have to save them!"
Superman said.

Superman grabbed his friends

just before Mongul reached them.

Soldiers came to help

as Mongul charged at Superman.

He pounded the Man of Steel

with his enormous fists.

Mongul caught Superman off guard.

"The first one's free, big guy,"

Superman said, getting to his feet.

"Let's see what you've got, puny being!"

Mongul roared.

Superman zoomed toward the villain.

SLAM!

Superman sent Mongul crashing

into a nearby building.

The building began to fall over.

It tumbled toward the crowd below.

Superman raced to the falling building

and caught it just in time.

"I'd better move this battle

to a safer place!" he said.

Superman began running

around Mongul.

He circled him again and again.

Superman ran faster and faster.

The Man of Steel created a

powerful cyclone.

The whirling funnel of wind

picked Mongul up off the ground.

Mongul went flying into space.

Superman followed Mongul into space. "Now I can stop you without anyone getting hurt!" Superman said.

"You cannot defeat me!" Mongul shouted.
The two powerful enemies clashed
in a cosmic battle!

With a blast
of his mighty super-breath,
Superman forced Mongul
back inside Warworld.

Superman used his heat vision
to destroy Warworld's engines.

Using his super-strength,

Superman heaved Warworld far away.

It disappeared deep into space.

"That ship is on a one-way trip!"

Superman said as he headed back home.

Earth was saved.

Back at the Daily Planet building,
Lois entered Clark's office.

"And where were you when I was on
the story of the year?" Lois asked.

"Like you said," Clark replied.

"I was just staring into space."